It's Raining Bats and Frogs!

ALSO IN THE JUNIOR MONSTER SCOUTS SERIES

Book 1:
The Monster Squad

Book 2:
Crash! Bang! Boo!

Book 4:
Monster of Disguise

JUNIOR MONSTER SCOUTS

#3 It's Raining Bats and Frogs!

By Joe McGee

Illustrated by Ethan Long

ALADDIN

NEW YORK LONDON TORONTO SYDNEY NEW DELHI

This book is a work of fiction. Any references to historical events, real people, or real places are used fictitiously. Other names, characters, places, and events are products of the author's imagination, and any resemblance to actual events or places or persons, living or dead, is entirely coincidental.

ALADDIN
An imprint of Simon & Schuster Children's Publishing Division
1230 Avenue of the Americas, New York, New York 10020
First Aladdin hardcover edition April 2020

Also available in an Aladdin paperback edition.

For information about special discounts for bulk purchases, please contact Simon & Schuster Special Sales at 1-866-506-1949 or business@simonandschuster.com.
The Simon & Schuster Speakers Bureau can bring authors to your live event.
For more information or to book an event contact the Simon & Schuster Speakers Bureau at 1-866-248-3049 or visit our website at www.simonspeakers.com.
Jacket designed by Karin Paprocki
Interior designed by Mike Rosamilia
The illustrations for this book were rendered digitally.
The text of this book was set in Centaur MT.
Manufactured in the United States of America 0220 FFG
2 4 6 8 10 9 7 5 3 1
Library of Congress Control Number 2019936823
ISBN 978-1-5344-3683-1 (hc)
ISBN 978-1-5344-3682-4 (pbk)
ISBN 978-1-5344-3684-8 (eBook)

FOR JACK

★★★★

I wish you were here
to read it.

· THE SCOUTS ·

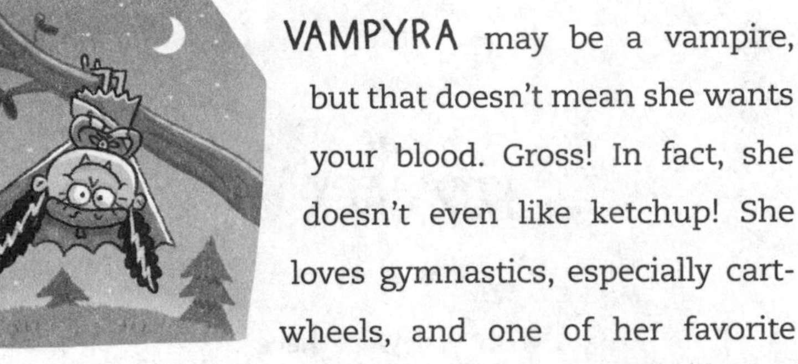

VAMPYRA may be a vampire, but that doesn't mean she wants your blood. Gross! In fact, she doesn't even like ketchup! She loves gymnastics, especially cartwheels, and one of her favorite things is hanging upside down . . . even when she's *not* a bat. She loves garlic in her food and sleeps in past noon, preferring the nighttime over the day. She lives in Castle Dracula with her mom, dad (Dracula), and aunts, who are always after her to brush her fangs and clean her cape.

WOLFY and his family live high in the mountains above Castle Dracula, where they can get the best view of the moon. He likes to hike and play in the creek and gaze at the stars. He especially likes to fetch sticks with his dad, Wolf Man, and go on family pack runs, even if he has to put up with all of his little brothers and sisters. They're always howling when he tries to talk! Mom says he has his father's fur. Boy, is he proud of that!

FRANKY STEIN has always been bigger than the other monsters. But it's not just his body that's big. It's his brain and his heart as well. He has plenty of hugs and smiles to go around. His dad, Frankenstein, is the scoutmaster, and one of Franky's favorite things is his well-worn Junior Monster Scout handbook. One day Franky is going to be a scoutmaster, like his dad. But for now . . . he wants a puppy. Dad says he'll make Franky one soon. Mom says Franky has to keep his workshop clean for a week first.

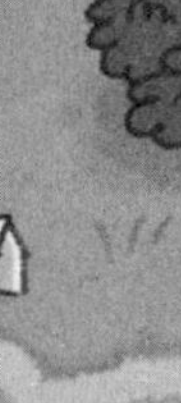

GLOOMY WOODS
LAKE
VILLAGE
BARON VON GRUMP'S HOUSE

CASTLE
GRAVEYARD
CROOKED TRAIL
WATERFALL

CHAPTER 1

"ON YOUR MARK," SAID FRANKY.

"Get set," said Vampyra.

"Float!" Wolfy said.

Franky, Vampyra, and Wolfy set their paper boats in the river and watched them sail away. It was springtime, and the April showers had made a wet, muddy mess of everything. Yesterday, the Junior Monster Scouts had raced frogs across the lily pads in the swamp. Today, they were racing boats in the river.

"Look at them go!" said Franky.

"I'll bet they go all the way to the waterfall," Wolfy said. "I wonder whose boat will win the race."

Franky and Wolfy ran along the riverbank, following the boats. Vampyra spun three times in a circle and *POOF*, turned into a bat. She flittered ahead of them, flapping her bat wings. She was practicing for her Flying Merit Badge.

"Come on, slowpokes," she said. "What's taking you so long?"

"No fair!" Wolfy said. "You can fly."

"And you don't have to run through this mud," said Franky. "It's slowing me down!"

"Excuses, excuses," Vampyra teased.

Wolfy dropped to all fours and raced

ahead of Franky. "Race you to the water-fall, Vampyra!"

"You're on," she said.

"Guys?" said Franky. But Wolfy and Vampyra pulled ahead of Franky and even ahead of the boats. "You go ahead," he said. "I'll just keep an eye on the boats."

The boats, however, did not need much keeping an eye on. They bobbed and swirled and raced along the river while Franky did his best to keep up.

The Junior Monster Scouts were not the only ones enjoying the light rain. The villagers were also celebrating spring. No afternoon showers were going to keep *them* inside. They put on their raincoats, rain hats, and rain boots, and they jumped from puddle to puddle with resounding *kersplashes*! They stomped and splashed and sang in the rain.

"Attention, villagers!" said the mayor. "I declare an umbrella contest!" He wiped the rain from his mustache. "Prize goes to the best decorated umbrella!"

"There should be a parade!" said Peter, the young piper.

"Quack, quack!" said the ducks, paddling about in a deep puddle.

And just in case you don't speak duck, "quack, quack" means *Yes, we should have a rainy day parade and an umbrella contest, and we will be the judges.*

"Oh, this will be splendiferous!" said the mayor.

• • •

But not everybody was enjoying the rain. Not everybody was excited about umbrellas and puddles and parades.

"Caw, caw!" said Edgar, Baron Von Grump's friend and pet crow.

"Yes," said the baron, "of course I—"

PLINK!

A big, wet drop of water fell from the ceiling and landed directly on the tip of his nose.

"Don't you think I know that we need another—"

PLINK! PLUNK!!

Two big, wet drops of water dripped from the leaky ceiling of the crooked old windmill and fell right atop Baron Von Grump's head.

"—bucket," growled Baron Von Grump.

"Caw, caw!" said Edgar.

"Well, don't just sit there. Grab an empty—"

PLINK! PLUNK! PLINK!!

Three big, wet drops of water dripped from the ceiling in three different spots.

"—pail," said Baron Von Grump.

He moved one bucket. *PLINK*. He adjusted a pail. *PLUNK*. He slid a can over to catch another drop. *PLINK*. He set one of his boots under a fourth drop. *PLUNK*.

Edgar hopped from beam to beam, pointing at new leaks and new drops.

"Caw, caw!" he crowed.

"Oh, confound it!" said Baron Von Grump. "Rain, rain, go away, come again . . . NEVER!"

PLINK, PLUNK, PLINK, PLUNK, PLINK, PLUNK . . .

Baron Von Grump glared at his leaky ceiling.

PLINK!

And caught a raindrop right in his eye.

CHAPTER 2

VAMPYRA FLIPPED AND FLITTERED AND fluttered along the riverbank. She was ahead of Wolfy. She was far ahead of their paper boats. And she was *very* far ahead of Franky. She was sure she was going to earn her Flying Merit Badge . . . as long as she could keep her wings going long enough. But right now, she needed a rest.

"Whew, flying sure is tiring," she said.

“So is swimming,” someone croaked from the edge of the river.

“Laguna!” said Vampyra. She landed and changed back into a vampire.

Laguna lived in the swamp with her mom, dad, and sixteen younger swamplings. But

today, she was not in the swamp. She was in the river.

Laguna pulled herself onto the riverbank and sprawled out in the wet grass. She stretched her webbed toes and spread her webbed fingers. Her gills heaved in and out. She seemed very tired. Even more tired than Vampyra.

"What are you doing in the river, Laguna?" Vampyra asked.

"Swimming lessons," Laguna groaned.

Wolfy and Franky finally caught up with them. They were out of breath too.

"I think I'm going to hurl a hair ball," Wolfy said.

"I think I swallowed a fish," said Laguna.

Laguna's mom popped up above the

surface of the river. She swam in circles on her back. She was an excellent swimmer.

"Hello, kids," she said.

"Hi, Mrs. Lagoon," they all answered.

"Laguna is going to take her swimming test today," said Mrs. Lagoon. "But first, she has a bit of practice to do."

"Mommmmm," said Laguna. "I can't swim to the other side."

"Sure you can," said Mrs. Lagoon. "It just takes practice, and for you to believe in yourself."

"You can totally do it," Vampyra said.

"I have a great idea," said Mrs. Lagoon. "Maybe Vampyra, Franky, and Wolfy will take lessons with you!"

"No way!" said Wolfy. "My fur will be a stinky, wet mess."

Franky shuffled his feet. "Um . . . my bolts might get rusted."

"I'd rather fly," Vampyra said with a grin.

"See, Mom?" said Laguna. "Even the Junior Monster Scouts are scared of swimming."

"Well, I wouldn't say we are *scared*," mumbled Wolfy.

"I would," said Franky.

Mrs. Lagoon floated on her back and blew a long jet of water up into the air. "There is nothing to be scared of," she said. "Besides . . . isn't swimming one of the Junior Monster Scout merit badges?"

Franky flipped through his scout handbook. Sure enough, swimming *was* a Junior Monster Scout merit badge.

"Come on, kids," said Mrs. Lagoon. "I'll help you all learn how to swim. You'll get your merit badges, and Laguna won't feel so scared with her friends alongside her."

Laguna sat up and clapped her webbed fingers. "Oh, will you?" she asked. "Will you? Will you? Will you? Puhleeaaazzze!"

Wolfy looked at Vampyra. Vampyra looked at Franky. Franky stared at his scout handbook.

"I suppose?" he said nervously.

Meanwhile, back in the village, the umbrella contest was well underway. There were bright umbrellas and striped umbrellas, umbrellas with swirls and spirals and flowers and polka dots. Tall umbrellas and short umbrellas, round umbrellas and square umbrellas.

"Oh, this is absolutely splendiferous!" said the mayor. "Truly wonderific! Everyone, get in line. The parade is about to begin!"

"Quack, quack, quack!" said the ducks.

They were very excited for the parade and even more excited to help judge the umbrella contest.

"Yes, yes, of course," the mayor said to the ducks. "You can join our parade as well!"

The ducks fluffed their feathers and waddled into line.

"Quack, quack, quack!"

(That means *Thank you* and *We are very pleased to accept your invitation*. As you can see, these were very polite ducks.)

"Okay, Peter," said the mayor. "Lead the way!"

Peter picked up his flute and led the parade through the town. Rain boots squelched and splashed in puddles. Ducks quacked. And everyone—*everyone*—was singing in the rain.

Everyone but Baron Von Grump in his crooked, leaky windmill, that is. *He* was NOT singing.

And if you know anything about Baron Von Grump, you will know that he was not singing because he was *not* happy.

And if he was not happy, sooner or later (probably sooner) he was going to form a plan. A sinister, diabolical plan to make him happy . . . and everyone else *unhappy*.

CHAPTER 3

MRS. LAGOON WAITED UNTIL THE JUNIOR Monster Scouts had changed into their bathing suits before continuing Laguna's swimming lessons. The rain was light and warm and kind of refreshing. It was like being squirted with a hundred little squirt guns filled with warm water. Except not in your eye, because nobody likes that.

Laguna waded out into the water until she was up to her waist. Franky, Wolfy, and

Vampyra stood at the edge of the river.

"Come on, guys," said Laguna. "The water feels nice."

Wolfy dipped his toe in. "Feels nice from right here," he said.

"Do any of you know how to swim?" asked Mrs. Lagoon.

"I can doggy paddle," said Wolfy.

"I can float," said Franky.

"I prefer to keep my wings dry," Vampyra said, turning into a bat and then back into herself.

"Laguna," said Mrs. Lagoon, "why don't you show the Junior Monster Scouts what you've learned so far?"

Laguna smiled. She had an audience now. Sometimes it's fun to do things when you have an audience. Sometimes they clap and cheer and say things like "Wow!" and "Way to go!" and "I wish I could do that!" That is exactly what happened with Laguna. While she swam back and forth, kicking her legs and moving her arms, Franky, Wolfy, and Vampyra were saying those very same things.

When she was finished, they clapped and cheered some more.

"You sure are a good swimmer," said Franky.

"Thanks," said Laguna. "But I still don't know if I'm ready to go out *there*." She pointed to the middle of the river. "I can touch the ground here. I can't touch there."

Mrs. Lagoon said, "If you can swim here,

then you can swim there. It just takes courage. And I'll be right there with you to help you if you get tired."

Laguna still did not seem convinced. It can be very scary to do something when you haven't done it before.

"I'd feel a lot better if the Junior Monster Scouts were swimming too," said Laguna.

She looked at Franky. Franky looked at Wolfy. Wolfy looked at Vampyra. Vampyra looked at her feet.

"Okay," said Wolfy, taking one full step into the water. "I can't believe I'm doing this, but . . . I'll take swimming lessons too."

"You will?" asked Laguna.

Franky gulped and stepped into the water. "Me too."

"Oh, yay!" said Laguna.

Vampyra sighed and stepped in next to them. "Ah, what the heck," she said.

"Oh, you brave Junior Monster Scouts!" said Mrs. Lagoon. "We'll have you swimming in no time. Now, the first step is . . ."

Mrs. Lagoon and Laguna began the Junior Monster Scouts' swimming lessons.

Baron Von Grump marched back and forth across the creaky floor of his leaky windmill. He placed a bucket here. He placed a bucket there. And with every new bucket, with every *plink* and *plunk* and *plink-plunk* of water, he grew even more grumpy than he already was. Edgar hopped from one leak to another, stuffing straw into holes. But

every time he plugged one hole, another one sprang a leak.

"Caw, caw!" said Edgar.

"Of course it keeps leaking!" growled Baron Von Grump. "It won't stop leaking until the

rain goes away. This old windmill—"

Baron Von Grump stopped talking. He stopped marching. He stopped placing buckets and pails. One side of his lip turned up, then the other, and suddenly he had the most sinister grin on his grumpy face.

"Caw?" asked Edgar.

"Yes, Edgar, I have an idea . . . a plan . . . a solution to get rid of this rain and splashing and singing and quacking."

See? What did I tell you? It was only a matter of time before Baron Von Grump had a plan. He was not at all fond of this frolicking nonsense. In fact, he did not like *any* celebration. He hadn't liked the village's cheese festival, or their 150th birthday party, and he was not about to start liking this springtime rain celebration.

Who celebrates rain? he thought. They should be indoors, staying dry and *quiet*. Quiet . . . What he wouldn't do for some peace and quiet.

Baron Von Grump slowly lifted his head up to the ceiling and stared past the beams, through a hole in the roof, to the giant wooden paddles of the old windmill . . .

PLINK!

. . . and caught a big old raindrop right in his eye.

CHAPTER 4

LET US GO BACK TO THE VILLAGE.

It was a grand sight to behold. Peter led a long line of villagers and ducks through the streets. They sang. They splashed in every puddle with their galoshes. ("Galoshes" is a fun and fancy word for rain boots. Try saying it. It's fun, right? Galoshes.) They twirled their umbrellas. The mayor wore his finest raincoat and his brightest rain hat and stood at the grandstand with several of the ducks, clapping and cheering for every umbrella that passed by. The mayor and the ducks had to judge the best umbrella, and it was very difficult because there were so many wonderful umbrellas of every shape, size, and color.

A small gust of wind picked up. It blew the mayor's brightest rain hat right off his head.

One very thoughtful duck tried to fly over and pick up the mayor's hat, but an even stronger gust of wind flipped the poor duck this way and that. She landed in a puddle with a quack and a splash.

"Oh dear!" said the mayor. "Hold on to your—"

The mayor was going to say "umbrellas."

He was going to tell everyone to hold on to their umbrellas, but before he could say "umbrellas," a superstrong gale of wind howled through the village and pulled umbrellas right out of villagers' hands. It flipped umbrellas inside out. Why, it even lifted one surprised villager right off her feet and would have carried her away if she had not quickly let go of her polka-dot umbrella!

It got windier.

And windier.

And so windy that it almost blew these words off the page.

"It's working!" said Baron Von Grump. "Flap harder, Edgar!"

Edgar would have replied if he could have. He would have said, "Caw, caw!" which would have meant "How much longer do I have to keep flying in circles?" But he could not reply. He had a string held tightly in his beak. That string was attached to a crank. That crank was attached to the giant wooden paddles of the old windmill. The harder he flapped, the harder he flew. The harder he flew, the faster the crank spun. The faster the crank spun, the faster the windmill paddles turned. And the faster the windmill paddles turned, the stronger the gusts of wind howled through the village, blowing hats off heads and umbrellas out of hands.

However, hats and umbrellas were *not*

what Baron Von Grump was trying to blow away. The rain clouds were. Each little spring rain cloud was being blown out of the village, pushed farther and farther away, until they were swept out entirely. They were pushed right out past the covered bridge, over the Gloomy Woods, and then, once they were far enough from the windmill, drifted toward the lake on their own.

With no clouds, there was no rain. With no rain, there was no reason for raincoats and umbrellas and certainly not for galoshes. The parade was over, the umbrella contest was canceled, and the villagers had no choice but to retreat to their homes. It was far too windy to stay outside without holding on very tight to something so that you did not blow away. The ducks couldn't even fly in this wind, and that made them very sad.

"Quack," said a very sad duck. That means *I wish it weren't so windy*, in case you don't speak duck.

Baron Von Grump listened. There was no plinking. There was no plunking. He slowly raised his eyes to the leaky windmill ceiling, but the leaks were gone. No drips or drops fell into his eye!

"Just a bit more, Edgar!" he said. "Let's make sure those rain clouds are pushed far and away for good."

Edgar flew harder and the crank spun faster. The paddles whipped around in a circle like a giant fan, blowing everything away from the old windmill and the

village. But poor Edgar was getting tired. Very tired. He was doing all the work. He was having a hard time keeping up with the windmill blades and the crank, since they were spinning so fast. On top of that, he was getting dizzy!

Edgar opened his beak for a very tired, very dizzy "Cawwwwww . . ."

And the rope he was holding flew out of his mouth. The windmill paddles kept spinning faster and faster, and Edgar couldn't stop them. He couldn't slow them down. Every single cloud was pushed away from the old windmill and the village, drifting out over the lake, where they began to form one . . . big . . . GIANT cloud!

CHAPTER 5

LAGUNA AND MRS. LAGOON SHOWED THE Junior Monster Scouts four swimming steps:

- Float.
- Kick.
- Crawl.
- Turn your head side to side.

"It's very important that you do not panic," said Mrs. Lagoon. "If you feel tired, or scared, just tread water. You already know how to do that. Just keep those feet moving like you're pedaling a bicycle and use your hands to spread little circles across the water."

"Like this?" said Franky. He waded in a little deeper and did just as Mrs. Lagoon had instructed.

"Just like that!" said Mrs. Lagoon.

"Show-off," said Vampyra. She splashed Franky and Wolfy.

"Look, Mom," said Laguna, "the rain is gone and the sun is out!"

"The clouds are all over the lake now," said Wolfy.

It was true. All the rain clouds had moved over the lake and were starting to clump together, one by one.

"Well, it looks like a perfect afternoon for swimming lessons," said Mrs. Lagoon.

"And my swimming test!" said Laguna. She was feeling much braver with the Junior Monster Scouts in the water with her.

"I can't wait to see you swim out to that marker!" said Vampyra. "You'll pass your swim test in no time."

"I'll bet you'll all be able to pass that test before you know it," said Mrs. Lagoon. "Now let's get swimming. Laguna will help me show you each of the steps. Ready?"

"Ready!" said Franky.

"Ready," said Wolfy.

"Ready?" said Vampyra. She was not so sure.

But whether they were really ready

(like Franky), or kind of ready (like Wolfy), or somewhat, but not really, ready (like Vampyra), they all followed Laguna and Mrs. Lagoon a little bit farther out into the water.

First it was up to their knees. Then up to their waists. Then right up under their chins.

"Let's practice those strokes," said Mrs. Lagoon. "Make your body as light as you can, and float on the surface. Kick your legs, use your arms and hands to crawl through the water, and turn your head from side to side."

"Wow," said Laguna. "You Junior Monster Scouts sure are quick learners!"

It was true. Franky, Wolfy, and Vampyra were swimming back and forth while Laguna and Mrs. Lagoon cheered and clapped and said things like "Good job!" and "Way to kick those legs!"

They were having a wonderful time. A spectacular time! Splashing and swimming and laughing. The sun was shining and the birds were . . . not singing. That was odd. No birds were singing or chirping. No bunny rabbits were hopping along the bank of the river. It was a bit unusual.

But they did not notice. They were too busy having fun.

"Ready for your test, Laguna?" asked Mrs. Lagoon.

"I sure am," Laguna said.

"All you have to do is swim out to that floating marker and then swim back," said Mrs. Lagoon. "I'll be close by in case you need help." Mrs. Lagoon turned to the Junior Monster Scouts and said, "It's important to remember that you should never swim alone."

Laguna took a deep breath. She stretched her arms. She stretched her legs. Then she pushed forward and began her swim out to the floating marker.

"Way to float, Laguna!" said Mrs. Lagoon.

"Look at her kick!" said Wolfy.

"Look at her crawl with those strokes," said Franky.

"Look at her move her head from side to side to breathe," Vampyra said.

It was true—Laguna was doing a fine job and would be at that floating marker in no time. But those clouds over the lake? They were getting bigger and darker.

To be honest, those clouds are making me a bit nervous for Laguna and the Junior Monster Scouts. Gulp.

CHAPTER 6

THE RIVER WAS NOT THE ONLY PLACE the sun was shining. It was shining over the village, but the villagers could not enjoy it because the winds from the old windmill were so strong that anything not nailed down was whisked up, up, and away.

It's true!

An apple cart, a wagon filled with hay, even an old lady knitting in her rocking chair all flew up, up, and away. (Don't worry—the old lady knitting was saved at the last minute. One quick-thinking villager caught the end of her yarn and pulled her back to safety.)

The villagers had to bring all their cows, horses, goats, chickens, sheep, and pigs into their houses so that the animals did not blow away. And don't forget the ducks! The ducks had to squeeze in as well. And the village cats, and the village dogs. It was very crowded. It was also very loud. It sounded something like this:

"I QUACK sure MOO hope BAAA the WOOF wind MEOW stops OINK soon NEIGHHH COCK-A-DOODLE-DOO!"

But do you know where it was not crowded? And not windy? And not rainy?

Where the sun was also shining? That's right—in the creaky, crooked old windmill where Baron Von Grump lived.

Perhaps, dear reader, you are saying, "Here we go again. . . . Baron Von Grump has set his plan in motion. He's such a grump! And the village needs to be saved *again*. When will the villagers ever learn? And the Junior Monster Scouts will need to save the day." And you would be right! Of course the Junior Monster Scouts will have to save the villagers, but how? Isn't it exciting? Here we go again! Now back to our story . . .

Baron Von Grump stood at the wide-open window and looked out over the village. He drew a deep breath, first with his right nostril, and then with his left, and then, finally, with both of his nostrils.

"What a glorious spring day," he said. He scrunched his eyebrows together and glared at the village. "At last."

Edgar flew in a crooked line right to the corner of the room and collapsed. He was still very, *very* dizzy.

"Perhaps some music will make you feel better, eh?" said Baron Von Grump.

"Cawwww?" Edgar said.

"Yes, something zesty," said Baron Von Grump.

"Caw . . ."

"And lively."

"Caw!"

"Yes, yes! Something you can dance to!"

Baron Von Grump marched straight to the cabinet where he kept his sheet music.

"I've got just the thing," he said. He riffled through his music and held up one page filled with musical notes. "This? No!" He held up another. "How about—no!" He scanned a third. "Too slow." He pushed his face against a fourth. "Rubbish!" He looked at a fifth and a sixth and a seventh and said, "Too soft . . . too loud . . . too weird."

Then Baron Von Grump's eyes settled on something. Something that was sitting right there, in front of his face, the whole time. There, atop the cabinet where he kept his sheet music, sat a small, framed picture of a small boy holding a very small violin. That small boy had very big, bushy, black

eyebrows. It was none other than little Baron Von Grump. He did not look grumpy in the picture. He looked quite happy. He looked like someone had just given him a balloon, and a puppy, and a piece of cake with two scoops of ice cream and said,

"Here, have this whole pitcher of fizzy soda all to yourself."

Baron Von Grump set down all his sheet music and held the small picture. His eyebrows lifted and his lips did a weird thing that they rarely did: they smiled. Not a sinister smile, or a sneer, or a mischievous grin, but a genuine smile . . . as if someone had given *this* Baron Von Grump a balloon, and a puppy, and a piece of cake with two scoops of ice cream and said, "Here, have this whole pitcher of fizzy soda all to yourself."

"Look at you, you handsome devil," he said to the framed picture of himself. "That was the day you finally learned to play your first complete violin song. A song *you* wrote . . ."

"Caw?" asked Edgar.

"Yes, it's quite zesty," Baron Von Grump said.

"Cawww?"

"Very lively." Baron Von Grump set the framed picture down.

"Caw caw?"

"You can certainly dance to it." Baron Von Grump tugged at his beard. "That's it, Edgar! That's exactly what I'll play. That will be the perfect song to make you feel better. Now where did I put that sheet music?"

He searched through his cabinet until he found what he was looking for.

"Eureka!" Baron Von Grump held the page of musical notes up over his head. "I found it!"

Just then the windmill tilted to the left.

Baron Von Grump stumbled. It tottered to the right. He staggered. The shutters swung open and closed. The cabinet slid this way. His stuffed chair slid that way. Baron Von Grump dropped the music and wrapped his arms around a beam to keep from sliding or falling or getting knocked over by the shifting furniture.

"What is going on?" cried Baron Von Grump.

"Caw!"

Edgar was right. The windmill paddles were out of control. They had not stopped. They had not even slowed down. They were going faster and faster. They were going so fast that they were moving the windmill this way and that!

Baron Von Grump reached out for his page of sheet music, the one with his first song on it, but a chest slid across the floor and flicked it into the air. Then a coatrack slid over and knocked the music toward the window. And then the shutters swung back and forth and pushed that music right out the window.

"NOOOOO!" said Baron Von Grump.

But it was too late. The music was gone and the windmill paddles were not slowing down.

CHAPTER 7

LAGUNA WAS HAVING A MUCH BETTER time than Baron Von Grump. She felt way better, a lot more confident, with her friends there. If they could jump into the river and learn to swim, then she could pass her swim test, she thought.

Laguna swam just like her mom had taught her, and before she knew it, she had reached the floating marker.

"I did it!" Laguna said.

Vampyra whistled. Franky clapped. Wolfy howled. They were very excited for Laguna.

"Okay, Laguna," Mrs. Lagoon said, "now swim back."

But suddenly . . .

The sky got dark. The air grew windy. And the first few drops of rain spattered down over the river.

"That does *not* look good," said Wolfy. He was looking out toward the lake, and he was right. It did *not* look good, not good at all.

All the little clouds were mashed into one big, supersized monster cloud right over the center of the lake.

"Listen to that wind!" said Vampyra.

The wind roared like a hundred—no . . . a thousand—a thousand tractor trailers rushing by on the highway. A thousand tractor trailers filled with hungry, roaring lions. And each of those lions had a bull-horn to roar through. That's how loud the wind was! Trees bent waaaaay over, their tops almost brushing the ground. And the waves! Oh, the waves . . . The water was a churning, choppy mess. It was a very good thing that Laguna, Vampyra, Franky, and Wolfy were not swimming in the lake.

"I've never seen so much rain!" Franky said. "It's all coming down over the lake."

That giant gray rain cloud was pouring so much rain on the lake that it was hard to see to the other side. No umbrella, no matter how big or how fancy, would have kept any villager dry in that rain. There was so much rain that the water was beginning to get close to overflowing, like a bathtub when the water keeps running and running and running and—

CRACK!

SLAM!

THUD!

Remember those trees that were bending over in the wind? Their tops almost brushing the ground? The roaring winds pushed two of those trees so hard that they broke right in half and fell at the mouth of the river, one after the other, piling together until they stopped most of the water from flowing.

The rain kept falling, the lake water kept rising, and now the water had nowhere to go but up. It could not flow into the river and out of the lake. It started to get deeper, and it started to trickle over the banks.

The water kept rising . . .

. . . and RISING . . .

. . . **AND RISING** . . .

"The lake is going to flood the village if we don't do something!" said Vampyra.

"We have to clear those trees!" Laguna said.

And she was right. If they could just clear those trees, the lake water could drain into the river and flow away.

"If the rain doesn't let up, I'm not so sure that anything will stop the lake from flooding the village," Mrs. Lagoon said.

Something landed in the river with a *KERSPLASH*!

"It's a duck!" said Franky.

"Quack."

Remember how I told you that it was so windy in the village that the ducks could not even fly? Well, that did not stop this particular duck from trying.

"Quack, quack," she said. That means *Don't worry, I'm okay.*

"Where are the rest of your friends?" Wolfy asked.

Annabelle (that was the name of this brave duck) told them all about the parade and the umbrella contest and the wind and finally . . .

"Quack quack quack quack *quack*!"

"The old windmill?" asked Wolfy.

"Out of control?" Vampyra said.

"Baron Von Grump must be behind this!" said Franky.

"We've got to stop the windmill and clear the trees that are blocking the river," said Laguna.

Mrs. Lagoon put her webbed hand out. Franky put his hand atop hers. Then Wolfy, then Franky, then Laguna, and finally Annabelle. One hand atop another (and a wing).

"Let's save the village," said Mrs. Lagoon. "I have a plan."

See? These villagers needed saving *again*. Are you surprised? Of course you

aren't. You already knew they'd have to be saved, but that's why you're reading, aren't you? To see *how* the Junior Monster Scouts will save the day. You want to see the Junior Monster Scouts in action! Well, so do I! Let's read on. . . .

CHAPTER 8

MRS. LAGOON'S PLAN WAS A TWO-PARTER. That means there were two things they had to do. Not one thing. If it were one thing, it would be a one-part plan. This was a two-part plan, and these two things were:

- Clear the trees so that the lake did not overflow and flood the village.
- Break up the giant rain cloud so that the water stopped rising.

"It's going to take all of us to clear those trees," said Mrs. Lagoon. "Except for Vampyra."

"I want to help!" Vampyra said.

"You have a *very* important job, Vampyra," said Mrs. Lagoon.

"I do?" asked Vampyra.

"You do," Mrs. Lagoon said. "You have to fly to the windmill and try to stop it."

"But that won't make the clouds go away," said Wolfy. "They'll still be there."

Franky twisted his bolts (he did this when he was thinking) and said, "Maybe if Vampyra can make the windmill go the *other* way, it will pull the clouds back—"

"And break them up when they hit the paddles!" said Laguna.

"This is an excellent plan," said Mrs. Lagoon.

Vampyra did not look so sure.

"I don't know if I can fly through all that wind," she said.

Laguna put her arm around Vampyra. "You sure can! I didn't think I could swim out to the middle of the river, but you, Wolfy, and Franky gave me courage."

"Yeah, Vampyra," said Wolfy. "You can totally do it!"

"And I'll bet that's just the thing that earns you your Flying Merit Badge!" Franky said.

I know what you're thinking. . . . You're thinking, *ANOTHER merit badge?* Well, of course. What kind of scouts would they be if they were not earning merit badges? I'll bet you would like a merit badge. Perhaps you deserve a Good Reader Merit Badge? Or an Honorable Junior Monster Scout Merit Badge?

"You're right," said Vampyra.

"And we'll clear those trees," said Laguna.

"By paw or claw, by tooth or wing, Junior Monster Scouts can do anything!" Franky and Wolfy said together.

"Wish me luck," said Vampyra.

She shimmered. She shifted. And suddenly, she was a bat. A happy, flappy, little black bat.

"There she goes!" said Franky.

Wolfy cheered her on with his longest and loudest howl.

"Quack!" said Annabelle. That means *Wait . . . I'm coming with you!*

And she did. Annabelle flapped and pushed through the winds in pursuit of Vampyra.

"Now let's clear those trees," said Mrs. Lagoon.

But clearing the trees was going to be no easy task! The water was very choppy and very deep. You would have to be a strong swimmer in order to stay in that water. Franky and Wolfy were *not* strong swimmers.

But that was okay because in order to clear the trees, someone would have to stand on the shore and push while someone else stayed in the water and pulled. It was team-

that water and only one little drain for it to go down.

Franky and Wolfy peered out toward the old windmill.

"You can do it, Vampyra," Franky said.

Wolfy howled again.

CHAPTER 9

VAMPYRA AND ANNABELLE FLAPPED AND fluttered and flew through the wind. It tossed them THIS way and THAT way

and THIS way and THAT way.

And just when Vampyra thought that maybe she couldn't reach that old windmill, she heard a loud howl.

"Wolfy!" she said. "I'll bet Wolfy and Franky are cheering us on!"

"Quack!" said Annabelle.

"That's right," said Vampyra. "We're almost there."

Vampyra and Annabelle flew over the covered bridge. They flew over the village. They flew across the fields and straight for the old windmill. The blades were going faster and faster, and the windmill was rocking back and forth. The closer Vampyra and Annabelle flew, the stronger the wind. The stronger the wind, the harder it was to fly.

"Just . . . a . . . little . . . closer," said Vampyra. She flapped her wings as fast as she could. It was almost as if she was flying in place.

But sometimes things are not that easy.

Sometimes if you really want to do something, you have to work a little harder than normal. And that is exactly what Vampyra and Annabelle did.

Meanwhile, inside the old windmill, Baron Von Grump held on for dear life. First the music sheets blew out the window. Then it was his plates and spoons. Then his sock collection. Then his shoes. Then the socks on his feet. Everything was blowing out the window. Even Edgar was blown right out the window!

"Cawwwwwwwwwwwww!!!!"

"Make. It. STOP!" cried Baron Von Grump.

Edgar snatched the rope in his beak. You remember the rope, right? The rope that

was connected to the crank? The crank that was connected to the paddles of the windmill? Well, Edgar grabbed right ahold of that rope and spun around and around and around and around with the windmill.

Poor Edgar.

"Look, Annabelle!" said Vampyra. "That's how we'll stop the windmill."

"Quack!" said Annabelle.

Vampyra and Annabelle flapped as hard as they could. They flew as fast as they could. They gritted their teeth and squinted their eyes and pushed. If they could just reach that rope!

Just . . .

. . . a little . . .

. . . bit . . .

Together, Vampyra, Annabelle, and Edgar pulled. And PULLED. And **PULLED** so hard that the windmill began to slow down. Slower. Slower. Slowwwerrrrr. Until finally, it stopped.

"Caw," said Edgar.

"Quack," said Annabelle. That means *No problem.*

Vampyra peered back over the lake. The big, dark rain cloud was still pouring rain.

"Okay," said Vampyra. "There's one more thing to do. Edgar, will you help us?"

Edgar squinted his eyes. He was not so sure he wanted anything more to do with this windmill.

"Caw?"

"Because the villagers are in danger," said Vampyra.

Edgar thought about this for a moment. Getting the villagers to be quiet was one thing, but being in danger was something else entirely. He certainly did not want to *hurt* the villagers, and he was sure that Baron Von Grump did not want to do that either. Besides, Edgar was tired of rain and tired of being dizzy.

Edgar shrugged. "Caw?" That means *Why not?*

"All we have to do," said Vampyra, "is make the windmill go the other way really fast. Instead of pushing the air, it will *pull* the air. That will get rid of that cloud for good. Ready?"

"Quack!"

"Caw!"

Baron Von Grump had just let go of the beam he was holding. He had just stopped being dizzy. He had just found a new pair of socks, when the old windmill started creaking and rocking and swaying again. And instead of everything blowing *out*, things were starting to blow *in*! A newspaper, a hat, an old pair of his socks . . . even a frog!

Baron Von Grump rushed to the window and looked up at the blades.

The first thing he saw was Vampyra, flittering outside his window.

"Hey there, Baron," she said, flashing him a pointy-toothed smile.

“Why, you Junior Monster Sco—”

Baron Von Grump did not finish his angry yelling. It’s hard to finish your angry yelling when a frog blows right into your mouth.

“Ribbit.”

CHAPTER 10

THE PLAN WAS WORKING!

The faster the windmill spun in the opposite direction, the more the big, dark, stormy rain cloud was pulled away from the lake. The windmill pulled the cloud over the village. It pulled the cloud right over top of itself, where it hung for a moment, pouring down buckets of rain. Rain ran down the roof. Rain poured out of the gutters. Rain pooled around the old windmill like a castle moat, and then . . . the cloud was pulled straight through the spinning blades of the old windmill and *SPLOOSH*!

That big ol' rain cloud broke up into a hundred little, fluffy clouds, which drifted along like lazy lily pads. Even the sun found a nice place in the sky to stretch out its rays.

One by one, the villagers opened their doors.

"The wind is gone!" they said.

One by one, they peeked their heads out.

"The rain has stopped!" they said.

One by one, they slipped on their galoshes.

"Look at those puddles!"

And one by one, they stepped outside and jumped from puddle to puddle. (Really, what good are galoshes if you can't jump in puddles with them?)

With the storm gone, the villagers could come outside and have fun!

Vampyra and Annabelle flew back down to the village. Edgar, on the other hand, had had enough. First cranking this way and then cranking that way? His feathers were flat-out exhausted. He collapsed on the rickety roof of the old windmill, drying his feathers.

Baron Von Grump spit the frog out of his mouth.

"Ribbit!" said the frog. That means *Thank you!*

Baron Von Grump tugged at his beard. He pulled at his hair. He had a pretty good idea of who had foiled his plan. He had a pretty good idea of who was to blame for all of this mess.

He lifted his spyglass to his eye and peered out over the village. He saw exactly who he'd suspected of ruining his plan. It was that furry wolf boy, and the large one with the bolts in his neck. And that batty girl with the pointy teeth.

"Why, you Junior Monster Scouts!" he hollered. "You have foiled me for the last time!"

He shook his fist. He stomped his feet. But nobody heard him. They didn't hear one word! Not the Junior Monster Scouts, not the villagers, not even the ducks. How could they have heard anything? They were too busy splashing in puddles with their fancy galoshes. They were too busy quacking and cheering. It's hard to hear angry ranting when quacking and galoshes are involved.

No sooner had Franky and Wolfy reached the village than a bright rainbow appeared in the sky. It started from the middle of the lake, where Laguna and Mrs. Lagoon were having a celebration swim, and stretched all the way over the covered bridge, over the village, and right into the window where Baron Von Grump stood ranting.

"Oh, look," said the mayor. "The baron is waving at us. Everyone wave to the baron!"

But Baron Von Grump was not waving. Baron Von Grump was blindly trying to feel for the windowsill. The rainbow was

so bright, and so blinding, and right in his eyes. He could not see a thing! He reached this way. He reached that way. He reached too far . . . and fell out of his window, landing with a *SPLASH* in the giant puddles around his windmill.

"Quack," said a duck, swimming circles around Baron Von Grump.

"Ribbit," said a frog, leaping atop Baron Von Grump's head.

Baron Von Grump waved a white sock.

"I surrender," he moaned.

CHAPTER 11

"OH, HELLO, JUNIOR MONSTER SCOUTS!" said the mayor. "Have you come to play in the puddles with us?"

"Actually," said Vampyra, "we were making sure everyone was okay."

"Yeah," said Franky. "Wolfy and I helped Laguna and Mrs. Lagoon clear the river so it would not flood the village."

"And Vampyra and Annabelle used the old windmill to clear the rain clouds," said Wolfy.

The mayor clapped his hands together. "Oh, splendid! Splendid, indeed! Thank you, Junior Monster Scouts! As a token of our appreciation, we, the villagers, would like to present you each with a pair of your very own galoshes!"

"Really?" said Wolfy.

"For us?" said Vampyra.

"Cool!" said Franky.

Before they left, the Junior Monster Scouts stayed for a few splashes of their own. After all, when someone gives you gift galoshes, it's quite rude *not* to make a few splashes. But then they were off, back to Castle Dracula, for that night's Junior Monster Scout meeting.

"Good-bye, villagers!" they said. "Good-bye, Annabelle. Good-bye, ducks!"

"Good-bye!" said the villagers.

"Quack!" said the ducks.

Off they marched in their new galoshes, down the road, jumping and splashing in every puddle they saw. They hopped across the covered bridge. They waded along the bank of the river and stopped to say good-bye to Laguna and Mrs. Lagoon.

"Congratulations on passing your swimming test, Laguna!" they said.

"Thank you, Junior Monster Scouts, for helping me feel brave enough and confident enough!" Laguna said.

"Come by for a swim anytime," Mrs. Lagoon said.

• • •

Franky, Wolfy, and Vampyra were so proud of their new galoshes that they wore them to that night's Junior Monster Scout meeting.

"What's with the galoshes?" said Wolf Man.

Franky, Vampyra, and Wolfy took turns telling Dracula, Wolf Man, and Frankenstein what had happened that afternoon.

"And you learned how to swim?" asked Dracula.

"You learned how to swim even though you were scared?" asked Wolf Man.

"Sounds to me like you three earned your Swimming Merit Badges," said Frankenstein. He pinned their badges onto their sashes.

"*And* your Bravery Merit Badges," said Wolf Man.

"For doing something even when you

were afraid," said Dracula. "That takes real courage."

Frankenstein pinned the Bravery Merit Badges on the Junior Monster Scouts' sashes.

"Wow," said Vampyra. "Our sashes are getting pretty full of merit badges!"

"Hope you have room for this one," said Vampyra's mom, Vampirella. She fluttered in the castle window in her bat form and then

shimmered and shifted and appeared before Vampyra in her vampire form. "You, my dear, earned your Flying Merit Badge."

"Way to go, Vampyra!" said Wolfy.

"We knew you could do it!" said Franky.

"Can I lead us in the Junior Monster Scout oath?" Vampyra asked.

"Of course," said Vampirella.

Vampyra cleared her throat and began:

"I promise to be nice, not scary."

Franky, Wolfy, and the rest of the monsters joined in.

"To help, not harm. To always try to do my best. I am a monster, but I am not mean."

Franky, Wolfy, and Vampyra recited the last line, hand in hand.

"I am a Junior Monster *Scout*!"

CHAPTER 12

BARON VON GRUMP KNEW JUST WHAT he needed to cheer himself up.

"I know just what I need to cheer myself up," he said.

See? I told you he knew. He was cold and soggy and very tired.

"A nice bubble bath," he said. "A nice, warm bubble bath will cheer me up!"

Baron Von Grump turned on the hot water. He poured in the bubbles. And while the water ran, Baron Von Grump gathered his tub things.

He gathered his robe. He gathered his slippers. He gathered a fresh towel and a long-handled scrub brush for washing his back. He gathered his bar of soap and his bath pillow and his favorite toy boat.

"Nothing like a warm bubble bath to relax," he said.

"Quack!" said a duck.

"Quack! Quack!" said two more ducks.

"Quack! Quack! Quack! Quack!" said a whole bunch of ducks.

A whole bunch of ducks swimming in Baron Von Grump's bathtub. A whole bunch of ducks playing in Baron Von Grump's bubbles.

You might say that Baron Von Grump was in a very *fowl* mood.

"Very funny. I'll bet you're just *quacking* yourself up, aren't you?"

Quack.

(That means *The End*.)

· ACKNOWLEDGMENTS ·

If you've read my acknowledgments in books 1 and 2 (*The Monster Squad* and *Crash! Bang! Boo!*), then you may recall some similarities. If you have not, you should go back and read them. There's going to be a test. A test on the content of the acknowledgments will occur in just a few short seconds. I'll wait.

Okay, good, you're back. We can start.

What is the square root of purple?

How many avocados does the Statue of Liberty weigh?

Why did the rhinoceros cross the river?

How'd you do? Feel good about it? Well, guess what? You passed! So now I can acknowledge people:

As always, I am so grateful for the love, support, and encouragement from my wife, best friend, fellow children's author, and adventuring partner, Jessica. She not only champions me and my work, but also challenges me and inspires me. Thank you, love! I'm so happy to be on this writing journey together. Like, not just a figurative journey, but a literal journey. We just bought an RV, and we're going to do some road ramblin' and coast-to-coast exploration in it!

Mad respect and admiration for my superstar editor, Karen Nagel, and the entire Aladdin team. I know you love these books as much as I do, and you've really made my vision become something even greater than I anticipated. Thank you! Karen also came up with the *perfect* titles. Much better than mine. *It's Raining Bats and Frogs!* is so much better than *Book Three*.

Thank you, Linda Epstein, for your hard work and dedication to the project. You saw it was bigger than my initial idea and encouraged me to make something more of it. I really appreciate that. Hats off to you. I'm not actually wearing a hat right now, but if I were, I would take it off. I wear a lot of hats, so I'll just wear one tomorrow and take it off to you then, okay?

Many thanks to the amazingly talented Ethan Long for his fun, zany, adorable illustrations. Wow! I just want to hug those Junior Monster Scouts! What do you say, Ethan . . . plush figures, right? Action figures? An entire line of toys . . . yeah.

As always, thanks to the modern-day Brady Bunch Jess and I have: Zachary, Ainsley, Shane,

Logan, Braeden, and Sawyer—we know you're proud of what we do. Thank you.

To our fuzzy, new puppy, Pepper . . . we love you, cute face! Even when you get the zoomies.

Thank YOU, the readers . . . because without you, there'd be no book. Or maybe there'd be a book, but no reader. And what good is a good story without a reader? If a tree falls in the forest, and nobody is around to hear it, does it still make a noise? How much wood could a woodchuck chuck if a woodchuck could chuck wood? Anyway, thanks for reading my books! And thanks for loving monsters! I hope they excite, entertain, and inspire you!

Finally, a great big thank you to all of the librarians (media specialists), teachers, and parents who battle digital distractions every day